RUDOLPH
the Red-Nosed Reindeer

By Barbara Shook Hazen

Adapted from the story by Robert L. May

Illustrated by Richard Scarry

A GOLDEN BOOK • NEW YORK

Western Publishing Company, Inc., Racine, Wisconsin 53404

Here is a delightful version of the tale of Rudolph, the red-nosed reindeer—the little reindeer so well known in song and story. Accompanied by Richard Scarry's fresh, imaginative illustrations, this Little Golden Book will bring joy to every Christmas stocking. Any material in this book from the song RUDOLPH THE RED-NOSED REINDEER, copyright 1949 by St. Nicholas Music, Inc., is used by permission of the copyright proprietor.

Once there was a reindeer named Rudolph, who lived at the North Pole, in Toyland.

Rudolph was younger and smaller than the other reindeer there. They all had proud, tall antlers. Rudolph's antlers were only tiny stubs.

Worst of all, Rudolph had a nose that was big and bright red. It was so red it glowed in the dark.

Poor Rudolph! He wanted to be like the other reindeer
in Toyland. Oh, to have a small, brown nose, instead of
a big, bright, red one!

The other reindeer made fun of Rudolph and called
him names.

"Rudolph, the red-nosed reindeer," they teased over
and over again until tears glistened on Rudolph's large
red nose.

Sometimes the other reindeer made a circle around
Rudolph and sang:

> "Red-nose, red-nose,
> A funny sight!
> Big as an apple,
> And twice as bright!"

They kicked up snowballs with their tiny hoofs and
covered Rudolph with a blanket of white, fluffy snow.

All the reindeer loved to play games. They played
tree tag and snow slide and tumble bones.

But Rudolph was never asked to play. He stood behind
a pine tree and watched. He was very lonely.

Rudolph couldn't even play hide-and-seek with the rabbits. His glowing red nose gave him away every time.

Before Christmas Eve, Santa's elves posted a sign on the gate to Toyland.

"Santa's Team-choosing Time," the sign said.

All the reindeer were asked to line up at eight o'clock in the meadow. Santa Claus was coming to choose the team that would deliver presents to every good little boy and girl in the world.

The reindeer fairly danced with excitement when they heard the news. They pranced, and tossed their antlers, and pawed the snowy ground with their hoofs.

Each reindeer hoped he would be chosen to guide Santa's sleigh. It was the greatest honor a reindeer could ever have.

Rudolph sighed. He was ashamed to have Santa see
his bright red nose. So he decided to hide.

At eight o'clock when all the other reindeer had gone to the meadow, Rudolph hid behind a holly hedge.

His bright red nose blended in with the bright red berries, and the thick growth of leaves concealed the rest of him. No one would find him there!

In the meadow all the reindeer in Toyland, except Rudolph, stood in a line while Santa inspected them.

Santa chose carefully—only the fastest, the strongest, and the best reindeer would do.

"I think Dasher will be fine. He's the biggest reindeer," said Santa.

"Dasher," wrote his elf assistant in a big book.

"And Dancer is the strongest," said Santa, pulling his beard.

"Dancer," wrote the elf.

"Ho! Ho! Let's see," continued Santa. "Here's Prancer and here's Vixen. They make the smoothest landings on rooftops.

"Comet is the fastest, and Cupid is the most sure-footed," said Santa. "I pick them."

"And last," said Santa, "I choose Donder and Blitzen. They're best at twisting over tree tops and skimming over telephone poles."

The reindeer in Santa's team were very happy. They rubbed noses. They danced and clinked their antlers together.

Even the reindeer who weren't chosen were given good jobs. One was to try out electric trains. Another was to cuddle Christmas kittens.

The only reindeer without a job was Rudolph. He wanted to help, but he knew he would be laughed at. So he stayed hidden behind the holly hedge.

At last it was Christmas Eve. Santa's elves were busy packing the sleigh.

"I don't care if they do make fun of me," said Rudolph suddenly. "I want to help, too!"

He dashed from his hiding place behind the hedge, and went to find Santa. "There must be something I can do to help," he decided.

The night was bitter cold and a terrible fog covered all the earth.

Santa's elves kept bumping into each other as they hitched up the team. They could hardly see as they put on each bright red harness and tied each jingle bell.

To make matters worse, Dasher and Dancer were fight-
ing over who was to be lead reindeer.

"I was chosen first!" said Dasher, stamping angrily.

"But you always trip over the moon!" said Dancer,
kicking a fallen star.

Even Santa was cross. "We'll never get there if you
two don't stop quarreling," he said. "And where is my
Christmas list? Dash it all! I can't see a thing in this fog!"

Just then a soft red glow lit up the snow.

"Thank goodness," said Santa, suddenly jolly again. "I've found my list. Ho! Ho! I must have tucked it in my belt.

"Who brought this fine lantern?" asked Santa. "I must take it with me. Why, I can see perfectly now."

"It's not a lantern," said Rudolph, trembling. "The light comes from my . . . my nose."

"Rudolph, the red-nosed reindeer!" said Santa. "I'm certainly glad to see you. Your light will guide my sleigh tonight. I appoint you head of my team and number one reindeer in all the world!"

Rudolph held his head high. Proudly he pranced to the front of the team.

All the other reindeer bowed. Donder and Dancer helped Rudolph put on his harness, and Cupid gave him a beautiful sprig of holly berries.

Then down, down through the clouds and over the
sleeping houses, Santa and his team flew on that foggy
Christmas Eve.

And leading the whole procession was Rudolph, the
red-nosed reindeer!

So if you see a soft glow in the sky on Christmas Eve,
you can be sure that Rudolph, "the most famous reindeer
of all," is very near.